Charlie...

THE MERRY CHRISTMOOSE

A Story of An Unexpected Dream Come True

Written by John Sherwood

Illustrations by Blueberry Illustrations

This book is dedicated to my parents Walt and Joyce Sherwood… without whom I would not be the person I am today. You inspired me as role models and filled my life with adventure, creativity, laughter, love, support and inspiration. There are no words that could truly express my appreciation.

Love John

This is the Christmas Tree Forest near the North Pole. It's home to Santa Claus, Reindeer…and a little Moose…

...named Charlie.

Charlie has many friends to play with in the forest…like Buddy the Bear, Freddy the Fox and Sammy the Squirrel. One day when they were out playing, they found a note nailed to a tree. It read… *"Reindeer tryouts for Santa's Sleigh Team. 10 o'clock Saturday morning at the North Pole Playground".*

Reindeer tryout
for
Santa's sleigh team
10. o'clock saturday
morning at north pole
playground.

"Wow" said Charlie…
"I've always wanted
to fly with Santa Claus!
Wouldn't that be great?"

"It sure would!" said Buddy.

"I'd love to go!" said Sammy
"but I'm afraid to fly".

"You're all crazy"… said Freddy… "You'd never catch me up there flying around… it's too cold! And besides Charlie… you're a Moose not a Reindeer…and YOU CAN'T FLY!"

Charlie thought about it and said… "Well…I've always dreamt of flying with Santa, and I bet if I try hard enough, I could do it! And then I could help him deliver toys to good girls and boys all over the World!"

"What makes you think you can fly Charlie?"…said Freddy.

"I'm almost like a Reindeer…I've got brown fur like them don't I?" said Charlie.

"Yeah…you've got brown fur" said Buddy.

"So if Reindeer can fly…then I don't see why I can't!" said Charlie.

Freddy still thought it couldn't be done and said *"Brown fur and antlers don't make you a Reindeer Charlie…YOU CAN'T FLY!"*

"Well I think I can fly" said Charlie… *"and I'm going to those tryouts and I'm going to fly with Santa…and help deliver presents! You'll see!"* …and with that, Charlie went home to tell his parents about it.

Charlie was very excited as he told his parents about the tryout, but, after hearing his plans, his mother hoped he wouldn't be too disappointed if it didn't work out.

She said *"Charlie, we love you very much, but honey, you're a Moose and…well…I don't know of any Moose who has ever been able to fly".*

But Charlie was determined.
That night in his room he dreamt of the wonderful
adventure…pulling Santa's sleigh all over the World!
The next day, with his parents and friends
by his side, Charlie left for the tryouts!

When they arrived, there were several Reindeer running, jumping and playing as they waited for their turn to tryout.

One of them saw Charlie and said *"Hey look everyone…a Moose! Who ever heard of a Moose on the sleigh team?"*…and they all started to laugh at Charlie.

But Charlie never lost his confidence.
He knew in his heart that he could fly!

As he watched each contestant, Charlie
just kept picturing himself doing it...and
saying to himself *"One...two...three...
JUMP!... One...two...three...JUMP!"*

Just then...Charlie heard a voice behind
him. *"So who do we have here?"*....
Charlie knew right away who it was....

It was Santa Claus himself!
Charlie spoke right up, *"I'm Charlie sir…*
Charlie the Moose, and I'm
here to try out for your sleigh team".

"Oh I see" said Santa as he
scratched his long white beard…
"I don't believe we've ever had a
Moose try out before. Why do you
want to be on my sleigh team Charlie?"

"I've always wanted to help you deliver toys to good girls and boys all around the World Santa, to make them happy."...said Charlie..."I know I can fly and make your team Santa... I just need a chance to try out!"

"Ho Ho Ho...okay Charlie" said Santa..."You certainly have the Christmas spirit. You're up next...good luck!"

This was it! Charlie made sure he got a good running start… and then…as he neared the take off line he said to himself…*"One…two… three…JUMP!"*…and he leaped into the air! AND THEN….

PLOP!!...He fell to the ground. He had hardly gotten in the air at all.

Poor Charlie…he felt so sad. He really couldn't fly like a Reindeer after all.

Charlie's family and friends tried to cheer him up, telling him he had tried his best.

"It's ok Charlie" said his mother.

"You gave it a good try Charlie"…said Buddy, but, Charlie was still very sad.

Then Santa started to read the names of his new sleigh team.
Charlie listened, but he knew his name would not be read.
And when the list was finished, Charlie turned to go home.

But Santa wasn't done yet...he told the
crowd he had another announcement.

*"There is still a position on my sleigh team to be filled.
It is a very important job that requires
someone who is full of Christmas
spirit...courage...and a desire to
help others. I need a Co-Pilot!"*

Wow! Everyone was so excited!

"That would be the best job of all!" said Freddy....
"Riding right up there next to Santa!"

Santa silenced the crowd…*"Attention!…*
Attention everyone. My choice for the position
of Co-Pilot on my sleigh is….Charlie the Moose!"

"What?" said Charlie…Had Santa really called his name?
Was he really going to fly with Santa after all?

Santa brought Charlie up on stage and then spoke to the crowd...
"Showing up here today, as the first Moose to ever try out for my sleigh team, took a lot of courage, and many of you doubted that Charlie could do it. But Charlie had a dream, and he followed that dream despite what others had to say. He wanted to fly with me to deliver gifts to girls and boys around the world...and now he's going to do just that... not pulling my sleigh, but as my Co-Pilot!"

Charlie was so excited! He never thought he could actually ride in the sleigh with Santa! This was better than he ever dreamt it could be!

Then Santa gave Charlie a red scarf to keep him warm...and his very own Santa hat to wear!

And he told Charlie..."*This hat will show everyone that you truly have the Christmas spirit and that dreams really can come true if you believe in yourself*".

The crowd cheered for Charlie as Santa placed the hat on his head. His family and friends were so proud of him.

And on Christmas Eve, Charlie's dream came true, as he flew with Santa delivering toys to boys and girls all over the World! And from that day on, everyone referred to that little Moose as...

Charlie...The Merry Christmoose!

Charlie...The Merry Christmoose is the first children's book from author John Sherwood.

The story represents the importance of perseverance in pursuit of dreams...which certainly applies to the completion of this book, which has taken 20 years since John first conceived the story of Charlie while flying on a plane for a business trip.

Based on a stuffed animal bought as a Christmas gift for a dear friend, it marks a personal milestone achievement for John to bring this story to print.

It is with sincere hope that *Charlie...The Merry Christmoose* will bring a smile to children around the world at Christmas time, and inspire them to pursue their own dreams, as they share the adventure of Charlie accomplishing his in an unexpected way.

CPSIA information can be obtained
at www.ICGtesting.com
Printed in the USA
LVHW072355131222
735183LV00008B/117